may the ~ love b~ then ya ~

SHEROES
of the BIBLE

WOMEN OF THE OLD TESTAMENT

LAUREN L. NELSON

WestBow Press books may be ordered through booksellers or by contacting:

WestBow Press
A Division of Thomas Nelson & Zondervan
1663 Liberty Drive
Bloomington, IN 47403
www.westbowpress.com
1 (866) 928-1240

ISBN: 978-1-5127-0901-8 (sc)
ISBN: 978-1-5127-0902-5 (e)

Library of Congress Control Number: 2015913578

Print information available on the last page.

WestBow Press rev. date: 9/4/2015

Scripture quotations taken from the Holy Bible, New Living Translation, Copyright © 1996, 2004. Used by permission of Tyndale House Publishers, Inc., Wheaton, Illinois 60189. All rights reserved.

WESTBOW
PRESS
A DIVISION OF THOMAS NELSON
& ZONDERVAN

CONTENTS

ACKNOWLEDGEMENTS

"Oh Lord my God, You have performed many wonders for us. Your plans for us are too numerous to list. You have no equal. If I tried to recite all your wonderful deeds, I would never come to the end of them."

Psalm 40:5

All praise and glory to you, Jesus! Thank you for using me to share with children the lives of these amazing women from the Bible. I love following you – for there is so much adventure when I do.

I owe an enormous debt of gratitude to three people, without whom I would have never completed this book:

To my sister, Kristin Thebaud, whose refinement of my stories breathed life into them. Thank you for grasping hold of my vision from the very beginning and for spending so much time talking with me about, and wrestling with, how to share these incredible women's stories.

To my husband, Kyle, for helping me keep my perspective childlike and for encouraging me to continue writing when, at times, I wanted to quit. Thank you for your constant love and for always believing in me.

And last, but not least, to my beautiful daughter, Kyah, whose innocent question was the reason I wrote this book. Thank you for being you! Your joy, laughter and smiles bring such light to my life. "I love you a bushel and a peck!" May you be inspired by this book to become the brave and strong SHEro that God created you to be!

FOREWORD

This book was written after a conversation I had with my 7-year-old daughter, Kyah. We were on our way to church when she said, "Mom, I have a question...why are boys more important than girls?"

I was shocked! I said, "What do you mean?" Then she proceeded to say, "It just seems like God thinks boys are more important than girls because all we ever learn about in church are boys."

Her question ran through my head for the next few days. I wanted Kyah to know her importance as a daughter of God and for her to know that He values girls and has a great plan for their lives, just as He does for boys. There are girls all throughout the Bible and I couldn't believe she had only heard of a couple. The Lord had a personal relationship with each of these girls and He loved to watch them respond in faith and trust Him when He asked them to do something.

Over the next few weeks, I began to teach Kyah stories in the Bible about girls who trusted God and did amazing things because of their love for Him. Kyah treasured hearing about the way these girls lived. She begged me every night for another story. I couldn't write fast enough for her! Kyah wanted to be just like the girls in the Bible. She wanted to be a SHEro – a girl who is a hero. She wanted to be brave and courageous and to live her life for God.

That is how "SHEroes of the Bible" came to be. I pray that as you read these words you too will trust God with your life and know that He loves you. God has called you to be a mighty girl that trusts in His goodness and love —even in really tough situations.

INTRODUCTION

God used many girls in the Bible to do some pretty amazing things! We are going to take a journey with some girls who experienced God in their lives in a significant way. My hope and prayer is that you understand that God still does incredible things today and He wants to do them through you. God wants you to become a SHEro for Him!

What is a SHEro? Here are a few things that mark a SHEro:

Satisfied only in God – SHEroes want the Lord more than anything else in this world. They hunger and thirst for more of God, just like we hunger and thirst for food and water.

Heart to do what He asks – SHEroes find joy in doing what God asks them to do and they love to tell everyone what He has done for them.

Ears to hear Him speak – SHEroes listen to what God says in all situations.

Rescuer – SHEroes believe that God is their rescuer and they do not let fear stop them from helping rescue others.

Obedient to God – SHEroes let go of what they want so they can do what God says is best. They are brave and courageous as they trust God.

We are going to learn about some SHEroes who experienced hard stuff, but they chose to say yes to God and to trust Him to rescue and comfort them. At the end of this book, I hope your prayer will be, "God, you rescued those girls from some pretty scary situations. I know you can rescue me too!"

Let's give God all of our fears and ask Him to teach us to trust Him every day and every moment. Now, let's meet some SHEroes who lived a long, long time ago…

SHIPHRAH AND PUAH

SHEroes of Exodus 1

"...But because the midwives feared God, they refused to obey the King's orders..."

Exodus 1:17

A long time ago in Egypt, the land of the Pyramids, there was a group of people that God loved named the Israelites. Although Egypt was not their homeland, the King of Egypt liked the Israelites so much that he gave them some of his best land to live in.

While they were living in Egypt, God blessed them with so many children that it was hard to count them all. Each family had many babies and then those babies grew up and had many more babies. Before you knew it, the Israelites almost had more people than the Egyptians!

During this time, the King who loved the Israelites died and a new King took over. This new King was afraid that the Israelites were growing too fast and he thought to himself, "What if they decide to take over Egypt? I'll make sure that doesn't happen!"

The King made the Israelites slaves so they wouldn't get too powerful and strong. The Israelites were made to work hard day and night in the hot desert sun without being paid. They were forced to build the Egyptians' homes and kingdom. They had to make bricks out of clay that covered the ground and they were beaten if they didn't make enough. Then the Israelites were forced to deliver the bricks on heavy carts they pushed by hand. Doesn't that sound terrible?

Even though life was very hard for the Israelites, God continued to bless them with more and more children. The more they were hurt by the Egyptians, the more children they had!

When it was time for the Israelite mothers to give birth to their babies, nurses would come to their homes and help them. Since the King was afraid of how many Israelites there were, he called in two of the head nurses, Shiphrah and Puah, and he gave them this command: "Every time you help an Israelite woman have a baby, if it's a boy kill him, but if it's a girl let her live. That way we can stop them from becoming too strong."

The King wasn't worried about the women of Israel, just the men, because he thought the men were the ones who could form an army to fight against him. The King didn't know that Shiphrah and Puah would follow God's will and become SHEroes.

Shiphrah and Puah knew if they didn't do what the King told them, he might kill them. But they loved God more than they feared the King. Shiphrah and Puah knew that something must be done to stop this horrible order from the King and they knew that as nurses they were the only ones who could do anything about it.

Shiphrah and Puah were in charge of many other nurses who helped women give birth to their children, so they gathered all the nurses who they knew loved God and told them the King's terrible plan. The women bravely agreed to do all they could to save the children of Israel from being killed. They knew that every time they helped an Israelite woman and her baby boy, they were risking their own lives, but they couldn't stand by while innocent children were being hurt!

So each time that an Israelite woman gave birth to a baby, the nurses made sure to do all they could to help her deliver a healthy child – boy or girl. The mothers of the babies then risked punishment or death by bravely hiding their baby boys from the Egyptians.

One day, the King ordered Shiphrah and Puah into his palace. "Why are there still Israelite boys being born?" he thundered. They stood frozen and frightened. Finally they told him, "The Israelite women are so strong that the babies are already born before we get there!" And the King believed them.

Shiphrah and Puah and many nurses and mothers made the choice to trust in God in spite of their fear of the King and his people, saving countless lives, including a boy named Moses. Moses was later used to rescue his people from slavery in Egypt, and led the way for the greatest rescuer the world has ever known – Jesus!

Devotion:

What are some things you're afraid of? Shiphrah and Puah faced their fears together. Who is someone you can face your fear with?

JOCHEBED, MIRIAM AND THE EGYPTIAN PRINCESS

SHEroes of Exodus 2

"...She saw that he was a special baby and kept him hidden for three months."

Exodus 2:2

Jochebed was scared. Her people, the Israelites, were slaves and the King of Egypt wanted her young child dead because he was a boy and might grow up and take over Egypt. Thanks to Shiphrah, Puah and the rest of the women who helped save the newborn Israelite boys from death, her child was still alive, but in hiding.

Jochebed knew the Israelites were continuing to grow strong, and the King was worried that they would join Egypt's enemies and fight against Egypt. The King was furious and ordered his people to throw every Israelite newborn boy into the Nile River so that the boys wouldn't form an army and attack Egypt when they grew up.

She couldn't let this happen to her precious baby. The Lord had spoken to Jochebed's heart that there was something special about her son. So she called on her daughter Miriam to help, and together these two SHEroes worked to make sure that this baby boy would live and fulfill God's will for his life. The baby boy was Moses.

When Moses was three months old, his mother could no longer hide him because, like most babies, he would cry and make lots of noise. She knew the Egyptians would soon find him and kill him. So she prayed that God would tell her how to keep Moses safe. God gave her heart peace and helped her to trust Him.

After praying, Jochebed knew that the only place her son could possibly escape the King was in the very river that the King ordered the babies to be thrown into – the Nile River. The river was dangerous, cold and filled with crocodiles. But there was no other way to send her son to safety than to place him in a basket in the Nile River.

She stood at the edge of the river shaking as she prayed and placed Moses in a basket made of materials that would help it float and keep her precious boy from falling into the crocodile-filled waters. She trusted the Lord would keep him safe.

Jochebed then asked her daughter Miriam to follow the basket along the river as it floated by so she could help make sure Moses was safe. Miriam was only 10 years old and was so scared. She knew if she was caught saving Moses, the King would punish her. But she loved her baby brother, so she gathered up all of her courage and carefully ran alongside the river trying not to be seen. She was heartbroken as she heard his cries and couldn't comfort him.

It felt like hours, but Miriam finally saw the basket wash up on shore – in front of the King of Egypt's palace! She was terrified – the King was the very person that they were trying to save her brother from. But suddenly Miriam saw a beautiful princess, the daughter of the King of Egypt, washing in the Nile River.

The Princess heard a baby crying in the distance. She looked over to where some tall reeds were growing out of the river. Then she saw it: a basket hidden among the reeds. She slowly and curiously waded through the river to the basket. As the Princess opened the basket she saw that it was a baby boy! Surprised, she thought, "This must be one of the Israelite babies my father ordered to be killed."

The Princess was heartbroken as she looked at this crying baby. She immediately picked him up and held him in her caring arms. She named the baby "Moses," which means "taken out of the water."

She quickly realized that she had nothing to feed this child. Miriam was still watching close by and saw that the Princess might save her brother's life. She bravely walked over to the Princess and offered to find an Israelite woman who could feed Moses. The Princess was relieved and told Miriam she would pay money to whoever Miriam found.

With joy in her heart, Miriam quickly ran home and told her mother how God had rescued her brother, Moses! Jochebed's heart was filled with joy knowing that God had saved Moses and he would now be safe under the protection of the Princess of Egypt.

Jochebed fed and cared for Moses for three years, helping him grow healthy and strong. When Moses was 3 years old, Jochebed gave the ultimate sacrifice. She returned her little boy to the palace so the Princess could raise him as her own son. But even though Jochebed and Miriam missed Moses, they praised God for his kindness and protection over him. Jochebed knew in her heart that God had saved Moses for something truly special!

Because these three women listened to the Lord and trusted Him, Moses grew up to be the rescuer of all of the Israelites. God used Moses to free them from the Egyptians, part the Red Sea and bring them through the desert to the edge of their Promised Land.

Devotion:

Jochebed, Miriam and the Princess all trusted God even when it was scary, and God blessed them. Is there a situation in your life where you want to trust God?

Rahab

SHEro of Joshua 2-6

"...For the Lord your God is the supreme God of the heavens above and the Earth below."

Joshua 2:11

The Israelites were tired and discouraged. When Moses led them out of slavery in Egypt, God had promised them their own land, a land "flowing with milk and honey," but the desert they lived in was harsh. There was no milk or honey. Forty years had passed – many babies had been born and many old people had died, yet they still had not reached their Promised Land.

Throughout these 40 years, the Lord continued to provide for His people. He rained down food from the sky called manna for them to eat, and He even provided water through a rock! He told Moses to remind the Israelites that they were His chosen people. God said to the Israelites, "I chose you to be mine, not because of anything you have done, but because I love you." So they kept marching forward in search of their Promised Land.

Finally, in their 40th year in the desert, the Israelites came to the edge of a land called Canaan. Canaan was beautiful and unlike anything the Israelites had ever seen. This land was spacious and green with many large fruit trees. The Jordan River was nearby and provided plenty of water. Honey dripped from hives like liquid gold and countless cattle provided sweet, rich and creamy milk. This was indeed the land flowing with milk and honey! The people's eyes and mouths opened wide as they looked at the land stretched out before them.

There was only one problem...the land was owned by a group of wicked people called the Canaanites who worshipped fake gods and did wicked things to people.

The Israelites doubted how God would give them this beautiful land when such evil people already lived there. Fortunately, Moses' helper, Joshua, had an idea. He sent two spies into the land of Canaan to a city called Jericho. These spies had one job: to explore the land. They needed to find out about the city's water supply, how much food was there and to learn how big Jericho's army was.

When the spies arrived in Jericho, they couldn't believe their eyes! Two large walls encircled the city – and these walls were very high. The walls also had four large towers where Jericho's army stood watch for invaders.

The spies entered through the main gates pretending to be travelers from a distant land. Once inside, the spies could see that the city was well supplied with food and there was a river that ran through it that provided them with plenty of water. Jericho also had a King with a large army that protected it.

The Israelites had hoped to circle the city of Jericho and trap the Canaanite people inside until they ran out of food and water. But the spies could see that it would take months for the Canaanites to run out of supplies! The spies were very discouraged. They knew the Lord had given them the land, but their faith was shaken as they looked at all the problems they would have to overcome.

The spies decided to visit one of the homes located on the outer wall so they could easily escape. Their hope was to learn more about the city and its army. There they met Rahab, who ran a business for foreign travelers visiting Jericho.

While the spies spoke with Rahab, someone recognized the men and ran to the King of Jericho. They told the King that the Israelites had come to spy on their land and attack it.

The King was furious! He sent men to Rahab's home who pounded their fists on the door and yelled loudly, "Bring out the men who visited you! They have come to spy on our land and take it for themselves!"

The spies stood frozen – they had been discovered! They knew they would be killed if they were caught. Rahab quickly led the spies to the top of her roof where she was drying strips of cloth and she told the men to hide among the large piles. She placed her finger over her lips to tell them to keep quiet while she spoke with the King's men.

Rahab took a deep breath and slowly walked down the stairs of her home. She bravely opened the door and said to the men, "Yes I spoke to them, but I didn't know where they were from. They left a little while ago. If you hurry you might catch them!" The King's men left quickly in the direction Rahab pointed.

Rahab quietly climbed back up to the roof and whispered to the spies, "I know that the Lord has given you this land. Panic has fallen on our city because we have heard how the Lord parted the Red Sea for your people." Then Rahab declared, "The Lord your God, He is the true God of heaven and earth!"

She made one request of the men, "When you capture this city, will you please promise to take care of me and my family?" The spies promised that if she helped them escape and told no one of their plan, they would protect her and her family. She grabbed a rope and threw part of it out of the upper window, lowering the men to the ground on the outside of the city wall, so they could escape.

The spies returned to the Israelites to tell the exciting news: "The people of Jericho are terrified because of all that God has done for Israel. God is definitely going to give us Jericho!"

Then the Lord spoke to Joshua and gave him strict instructions for how to march around the city of Jericho for six days. On the seventh day, when they blew a loud and long blow in the trumpet, the high walls of Jericho would tumble to the ground! The spies had thought it would take months to enter the city of Jericho, but God said it would be done in just one week.

On the 7th day, when the trumpets blew, the walls of Jericho fell and the Canaanites were driven out. Miraculously, the portion of the wall where Rahab lived did not fall down and she and her family were rescued.

Because of Rahab's faith, she was invited to become part of the Israelites' family, all because she chose to believe God and trust Him even when no one else in Jericho did.

Devotion:

What does it mean to be a part of a family? How can you treat your friends and neighbors like family? Do you want to be part of God's family?

DEBORAH AND JAEL

SHEroes of Judges 4-5

"...Get ready! This is the day the Lord will give you victory over Sisera, for the Lord is marching ahead of you!"

Judges 4:14

The Israelites hung their heads in disbelief and shame. They were slaves again! They had left the slavery of Egypt and had come to their Promised Land but they were again made to work as slaves. When they defeated the wicked Canaanites and took the Promised Land from them, the Israelites foolishly decided to worship the Canaanites' fake god – a god they believed controlled the storms and weather.

They had learned the truth the hard way – the Canaanites' god was not real. The Israelites had now been slaves of the Canaanites for 20 long years and knew only their one true God could save them. But how?

Deborah knew just how to defeat the Canaanites because she was a friend of God and He told her exactly what to do. Deborah was a judge over the Israelites, which meant she was a wise leader in Israel. The Israelites would come to her home in the mountains for advice, and she taught them how to live right by loving each other and God with their whole hearts.

As the Canaanites grew more and more wicked, Deborah would sit in her mountain home crying out to God for help. She knew the Canaanites and their evil leader Sisera were trying to take the Promised Land that the Israelites had worked so hard for. Sisera led a well-trained army of men who rode iron chariots pulled by strong horses. He used his army to bully the Israelites every day, and it was working. The Israelites were scared!

But the Lord had spoken words of hope to Deborah. She came to Barak, the leader of the army of Israel, with a message from God: "The Lord said it's time to stand against Sisera and the Canaanites." Barak refused, shaking his head in unbelief and impatience at what seemed like a ridiculous statement – he thought they would lose! But she said again, "The God of Israel has told you to fight against Sisera. You are to gather your men and fight the Canaanites, and the Lord says He will save Israel."

But Barak still refused. He knew that his army was much smaller than Sisera's and they were not well-trained and did not have weapons or chariots. Barak was sure there was no way they would win the battle. In fact, he was so sure it wouldn't work that he said, "The only way I will go into battle is if you, Deborah, lead the army!"

To Barak's surprise, Deborah said yes! But she knew Barak did not believe God's words. So she told him, "This is the day the Lord will save the Israelites from Sisera. The Lord has gone before you to fight your battle. But because you did not trust God to save Israel, God will have a woman win the battle!"

So Deborah bravely walked onto the battlefield with all of the Israelite soldiers behind her. They gasped as they saw Sisera and his many chariots and horses, but they entered the battle believing God had spoken to Deborah. The Israelites were losing the battle when all of a sudden, God sent a huge storm to the land! It rained so much that the land turned into thick mud and all of Sisera's chariots could no longer move. The earth began to shake, and Sisera and his mighty warriors grew panicked and ran away in all directions.

The Lord showed Himself to be the one true God, in charge of everything, including the storms and weather! God used the weather, the very thing the Canaanites had worshiped, to defeat them.

As the rain continued to fall and Sisera's men scattered, Sisera quickly jumped off his chariot and ran to find the closest house so he could hide from the Israelites. A woman named Jael ran out to meet him. She was a Kenite and she and her family lived in tents near the battlefield.

What Sisera didn't know was that even though Jael was a Kenite, she was also a relative of Moses' wife, and she was on the Israelites' side.

Jael knew this was her chance to kill the evil Sisera and defeat the Canaanites. So she said, "Come quickly! You will be safe in my tent!" She knew she had to trick him by showing him respect. When he asked for a drink, she gave him milk and some meat to eat.

Sisera said to Jael, "Stand at the door and make sure no one tries to find me. If anyone comes, tell them I'm not here." She agreed and, putting a blanket over him, told him to lay down and rest.

When Sisera finally fell asleep, Jael knew that this was her only chance. She quietly tiptoed over to the sleeping warrior and killed him while he slept. When she saw Barak, the commander of the Israelite army, approaching her tent in search of Sisera, she ran out to meet him and tell him the good news: "Come and I will show you the man you are looking for!"

Barak couldn't believe his eyes! Deborah was right: The Israelites had defeated the Canaanites, just as the Lord had said, and the victory came through the hands of a woman! The Israelites were now free to live in peace and worship their God, all because of the bravery of these two women. Thanks to Deborah and Jael, Israel had peace for 40 years.

Devotion:

Have you ever thought negative thoughts about someone because of how they looked or what others said about them? How can you begin to see others with God's eyes of love?

RUTH AND NAOMI

SHEroes of the Book of Ruth

"...I have heard how you left your father and mother and your own land to live here among complete strangers."

Ruth 2:11

Israel had become a dry and thirsty land and the people were suffering. There hadn't been rain for many years, and the Israelites could no longer grow food or feed their animals. An Israelite woman named Naomi knew that soon she and her household would have nothing to eat. She had no other choice but to move her family to another land – a land where they might survive.

They soon found the land of Moab a good place to call home. There Naomi, her husband and two sons settled, and her sons married Moabite women.

Time passed and Naomi's husband and sons died – the three women grieved the loss of the men they loved. Naomi and her daughters-in-law were left alone to take care of their large property and earn enough money to buy food. Naomi knew she couldn't take care of her daughters-in-law, and told them to return to their families. As tears ran down her face, Naomi said, "I pray that God will reward you for being so kind to me and my sons. I pray you find new husbands and a new beginning." She kissed them, and the three women wept and hugged each other. One daughter-in-law returned to her family, but Ruth, her other daughter-in-law, refused to leave.

Ruth, gently but with strong conviction, said to Naomi, "Wherever you go, I will go. Your people will be my people, and your God will be my God." From then on, these two women formed a deep love and friendship with each other and they continued to live together in the land of Moab.

Soon, a man traveling through Moab told Naomi that rain had returned to Israel. Naomi was thrilled! She longed to return to her homeland. Once again Naomi told Ruth to return to her own family but Ruth again refused to leave her and together they moved to an Israelite town called Bethlehem.

The people of Bethlehem remembered Naomi and rejoiced at her return. Ruth and Naomi were welcomed with open arms. They had returned at just the right time! Everyone in Bethlehem was celebrating because it was the time of year they collected the barley, a grain used for cooking. The people of Israel worked hard all year long preparing the barley to be gathered.

Because Naomi loved Ruth, she came up with a plan to make sure she would be provided for – and it began with collecting barley. Naomi had a relative named Boaz who loved the Lord. He was very rich and owned many barley fields. Naomi told Ruth to gather the leftover grain from his fields and bring it home for them to eat. In Israel, farmers would allow orphans and widows to pick up the leftover grain as a source of food.

Ruth agreed and day after day the sun beat down on her back as she picked up the leftover grain in the fields. It was hard work, but Ruth was committed to making sure she and Naomi had enough to eat.

Boaz cared about all of his servants and would often come visit them in his fields. As he visited, Boaz observed Ruth working hard daily and knew she was dedicated to helping her mother-in-law. He was very kind to her even though she was a stranger from another land.

One day, Ruth sat down to eat after many long hours of laboring in the barley fields. Boaz's eyes followed Ruth as she sat – he could not take his eyes off of her! He admired her devotion and, with kindness in his eyes, he shyly approached Ruth and said, "I pray that God will repay you for your hard work and that you will find protection in His mighty arms."

Boaz told his workers to drop grain on purpose for Ruth to collect and bring home. That day she collected about 35 pounds of barley! When Ruth returned home to Naomi she told her all that had happened. Naomi shouted joyfully, "God has not forgotten about us!" She told Ruth to continue collecting grain and, for two more months, that is just what she did.

While Ruth worked in the fields, Naomi noticed something happen in Boaz. She watched him as he admired Ruth and she could see that he loved her. So she came up with another plan. Boaz was much older than Ruth and in their culture this meant that if they were to be married, Ruth would need to ask Boaz to marry to her.

Now, what happens next may seem a little silly to you and me, but it was common in Israel at that time. Ruth was to ask Boaz to marry her by laying down next to his feet!

So one night after dinner, Boaz laid down to sleep on a large pile of barley. Ruth dressed in her best clothes and was as beautiful in appearance as she was in her heart. She saw Boaz as he lay sleeping, and she quietly laid down at his feet. She was exhausted from her long day of working in the sun and soon fell asleep.

When Boaz woke up, he rubbed his eyes and couldn't believe what he saw: This beautiful woman was laying at his feet. Boaz knew by her actions that Ruth wanted to marry him and he was thrilled! He gently touched her shoulder and said, "You are a kind and good woman. You could have chosen a younger man, poor or rich, but you chose me and I am honored. I will make all the arrangements for us to be married."

Soon, Boaz and Ruth were married and God gave them a son. As Naomi held her grandson in her arms for the first time, she looked at Ruth and said, "Praise the Lord that He has not forgotten about us!" With huge grins on their faces, Ruth and Naomi giggled and joyfully thanked the Lord for all that he had done for them.

Devotion:

Have you ever felt forgotten by someone or known someone that feels forgotten? What are some ways that God shows us that He has not forgotten about us and how can you share that with others?

KYAH

SHEro of Judges 9

"...God punished Abimelech for the evil he had done against his father...and his 70 brothers..."
Judges 9:50

Israel had a judge named Gideon. He was a good man who loved the Lord and helped Israel follow God. Gideon had 71 sons — that's a lot of kids! One of his sons, Abimelech, was an evil man. Abimelech was prideful and worshiped fake gods. He wanted more than anything to be ruler of Israel but knew he was competing with his brothers. So he gathered some evil men and formed a plan to kill all 70 of his brothers.

Abimelech's plan worked, and when the last of his brothers was dead, Abimelech became ruler over Israel. Three years later, the Israelites couldn't take any more of his selfishness and violence. In the dark of night, they came together secretly to plan how they would kick Abimelech and his army out of Israel.

But Abimelech heard about the Israelites' secret plan. He was very angry that anyone would consider fighting against him. He shouted to his men, "Let's go to the town of Thebez and surround the city and attack it!" They circled Thebez and forced open the gates. Abimelech's army charged into the city and overtook it.

The men, women and children of Thebez ran for their lives to the top of a huge tower inside the city. They hid, hoping that the tower would protect them. All of the people of Thebez were frightened and held each other close, in hopes of protecting their loved ones from the horrible Abimelech and his mighty army. Among them was a girl whose name we never knew, so we will call her Kyah.

Just as Abimelech and his men were about to enter the door at the bottom of the tower, Kyah looked up and saw a gigantic rock placed in a window at the top of the tower. It was hanging just over the entrance where Abimelech was. She had an idea!

Kyah felt hope for the first time, as she realized she might be able to stop Abimelech and his men. Looking at the rock, she bravely left her family to run to the window. With all her strength, she pushed the large rock out of the window and it fell from the top of the tower and landed on the wicked Abimelech! When his army saw that he was dead, they all ran away in defeat.

The people of Thebez shouted and jumped for joy as they realized that their lives had been saved! God used Kyah to save the people of Thebez when everyone else was overcome by fear and did nothing. Her courage and trust in the Lord rescued God's people from the hands of their enemies.

Devotion:

Have you ever seen something happening that wasn't right and did nothing about it? What are some things you can do to help when others do nothing?

HANNAH

SHEro of 1 Samuel 1-2

"...If you will look upon my sorrow and answer my prayer and give me a son, then I will give him back to you. He will be yours his entire lifetime."

1 Samuel 1:11

In the mountains of Ephraim, there lived an Israelite woman named Hannah and her husband, who loved each other deeply. Hannah's deepest desire was to be a mother.

Hannah was sad because she ached to have her home filled with the joy and laughter of children. After all, kids are fun! She wanted nothing more than to hold and care for a child of her own.

Day after day, she watched her friends and family with their children. She would press her hands against her stomach and long to feel a baby kicking inside. But month after month passed, and Hannah was still not pregnant.

As if that wasn't hard enough, many women in her town said mean things to Hannah because she couldn't have children. Some days, she would lay in bed and cry over the things people said and often she couldn't eat because she was so unhappy. Though Hannah was very sad, she didn't lose faith in God. She believed the Lord was good and had a plan for her life.

One day Hannah went to the temple to tell God what was on her heart. She wept as she cried out to God, "If you will see my pain, will think of me and will give me a son, then I promise to give him back to you as a sacrifice, so he can serve you all the days of his life." Hannah gave the Lord her desire for a son and believed that she could trust Him. She wanted a family more than anything, but her love for God was greater than what she wanted for herself.

That day, when she left the temple, Hannah had an overwhelming peace that God was in control of her life. She placed her desire for a child in the hands of a God who was loving and kind, and her heart was lighter because of it.

Do you know what happened next? After a short time, Hannah began to feel a baby kicking inside of her tummy and she later gave birth to a son she named Samuel! Hannah cried happy tears as she held her newborn son for the first time. God answered her prayer and gave her the desire of her heart. She would not forget her promise to the Lord – to give Samuel back to Him when the time was right.

For three years, Hannah fed Samuel milk when he was hungry, held him when he cried and watched him take his first steps – her dream had come true! But when he was 3 years old, she knew it was time to bring Samuel to the temple so he could grow up in the presence of the Lord.

Hannah kissed Samuel and told him she loved him and would visit him as often as she could. They hugged once more and she left, trusting that God would take good care of her son – after all, God is the best parent ever!

As Hannah walked away from the temple, she felt great joy because she had trusted God and kept her promise to Him. She declared, "God, you are good! There is no one like you." Because Hannah trusted God, He multiplied her dreams. He didn't just give her one child, He filled her home with five more children – three more boys and two girls!

Hannah had faced such cruelty from women in her town, but she never doubted that God loved her and had good plans for her. Because of her faith, Samuel grew up in the temple knowing the love of his mother and the love of the Lord. In fact, from the time Samuel was a little boy, God spoke to him and used him as a prophet to remind the Israelites of His great love for them.

Devotion:

Is there something that you have prayed about for a long time? Are you still praying about it or did you see that prayer answered? What can we learn from Hannah about trusting God with our prayers?

ABIGAIL

SHEro of 1 Samuel 25

"...And when the Lord has done these great things for you, please remember me, your servant."
1 Samuel 25:31

Nabal was a selfish, angry and evil man. He didn't care about anyone and treated everybody horribly. He was, however, very rich – he had 3,000 sheep, 1,000 goats and huge fields of grain that stretched out for miles and miles.

Nabal had a beautiful wife named Abigail and she was the exact opposite of him – she was kind, gentle and wise. You may be wondering why she married such a wicked man! Well, at this time in Israel, women didn't choose the men they married; their parents chose for them. So Abigail was forced to marry Nabal because he could provide a home and food for her, but she didn't love him.

Little did Nabal or Abigail know, there was a brave man named David hiding in their land. He and his army of 600 men were hiding from the jealous King of Israel, Saul. Have you ever heard the story of David and Goliath? Well, David struck down a huge giant named Goliath with just a small stone because the giant was bullying God's people and calling God names. Later, God spoke to David through the prophet Samuel and said that David would be the next King of Israel. King Saul was terrified that David would take his kingdom away from him. He hated him and wanted anyone who followed him dead! So David and his men were hiding.

As it turned out, Nabal's land was a great place to hide, so David and his men lived there for quite some time. Day and night, David and his army protected Nabal's shepherds and those that worked in his fields. His soldiers were like a wall around Nabal's property, defending all that dwelled there from thieves and animals.

When the grain had grown big and tall, Nabal's many servants collected it for him. When the servants gathered more than enough grain, David sent 10 of his men to ask Nabal if he would share some grain with them since he had more than enough. After all, David and his men had protected Nabal's servants and property for quite some time – and they were hungry! Their mouths watered as they thought of all the soft and delicious bread they could make from a portion of the grain collected.

When Nabal was asked to share his grain, he laughed in the faces of David's men and said, "Who are you? I don't know you and why should I share my food with you?"

David's men returned to him discouraged and told him how terrible Nabal was to them. David was furious! Nabal was mean, rude and selfish and David could not let him get away with it. So he said to his army, "Everyone come with me! Let's go to Nabal's home and teach him a lesson!"

David was angry and, as you know, it is never good to make decisions when you're angry. David planned to hurt Nabal and everyone who lived in his house.

As David's men were preparing to attack Nabal's home, a servant boy ran desperately to Abigail for help. He was out of breath but managed to say, "David and his men asked Nabal to share his food but he was awful to them! They have been so kind to us and have protected us day and night. I know that David and his men will not let Nabal's actions go unpunished. Please go and talk to David and try to change his mind!"

Abigail quickly ran to her kitchen and began cooking enough food for David and his 600 men — wow, that probably took a long time! She made bread, sweet cakes, packaged raisins and meat and also prepared drinks for everyone. Exhausted after a long day of cooking, she climbed onto her donkey and rode as fast as she could to meet David before his army arrived at her home.

When Abigail saw David, she jumped off her donkey and bowed low before him saying, "Let this guilt fall on me! I'm sorry my husband treated you so horribly. I know that God has chosen you to be the King over Israel. Please don't do something evil because you are angry. God's the one who fights our battles!"

David was humbled by Abigail's words, and he knew she was right. So he said to her, "Go in peace. You and your household will be safe." Abigail was relieved and said, "When God does great things for you, please remember me!" David smiled sweetly and turned to leave with his men. They quickly rode to find a new place to hide from King Saul.

Abigail had saved the day! And do you know what happened next? God fought David's battle for him, just as Abigail had said. Nabal grew very sick and died. When David heard that Nabal was dead, he remembered Abigail's kindness, gentleness and wisdom and asked her to marry him. Because of her humility, Abigail became the wife of King David!

Devotion:

Have you ever made a decision when you were angry or seen others do the same? What are some things that Abigail did to help David when he was angry?

ESTHER

SHEro of the Book of Esther

"...Who knows if perhaps you were made Queen for just such a time as this?..."

Esther 4:14

Mordecai was a wise Israelite who was highly respected by his people. He even took the responsibility of raising his cousin, Esther, after her parents died when she was just a small child. Esther became like a daughter to Mordecai and grew to be a lovely young woman – everyone admired her beauty and she stood out among all the women in the land.

The Israelites lived under the rule of a Kingdom named Persia, and Persia needed a Queen. One day, the King summoned his servants to his palace and gave them these instructions, "Go into every village, town and city to find for me the most beautiful women in all of Persia." The servants immediately obeyed and began the search for their Queen. They were to gather the selected women and bring them to the palace to train them how to behave like a Queen. They were given fancy clothes to wear and were bathed in fancy perfumes so they would smell as beautiful as they looked. After one year, the King would choose his favorite of all the women to become his wife.

Esther was chosen, along with many other women, to live in the palace for one year. As she was leaving, Mordecai kissed her cheek and quietly warned her: "Do not tell anyone you are an Israelite. You could be treated very badly if you do." Esther was frightened and didn't want to leave Mordecai and the home she had come to love. But she obeyed her uncle and bravely left her family behind to live in the palace of the King.

Each day, Mordecai would walk through the city's courtyard near the palace gates to find out how Esther was doing. At the end of one year, the chosen women were presented to the King. When the King saw Esther, he thought she was the most beautiful of all of the women who stood before him. The King then made the announcement to all of the people of Persia that Esther would be his Queen. All this time, Esther kept her identity a secret from the King and his servants. No one in the palace knew she was an Israelite.

Soon after Esther was made Queen of Persia, one of the King's most respected men, Haman, was riding through the kingdom. Everyone bowed low to honor him, except for one man – Mordecai. He knew the truth about Haman, that he was an evil man who hated the Israelites and wanted them driven out of Persia. So Mordecai stood tall with his head held high and refused to bow.

Haman was furious that someone would refuse to bow before him, especially an Israelite! He went to the King and said, "The Israelites live by different laws and do not obey or respect the laws of Persia. They think they're better than us so we should rid the kingdom of them."

The King agreed to the plan and Haman smirked and said to himself, "Now we'll see if the Israelites still smile and hold their heads high!" He ordered that in a year's time, his soldiers should kill all of the Israelites and take everything they owned.

Little did Haman know, Mordecai had discovered his plot and sent a message to warn Esther. The message read, "Esther, you must do something! Your people are in danger. Maybe the Lord made you the Queen of Persia in order to save our people!"

Esther was terrified. She knew she could be killed because she too was an Israelite. She wrote a reply to Mordecai's message: "You know that anyone who goes to speak to the King without his permission could be killed!"

But suddenly a peace came upon Esther and she knew what she had to do – trust the Lord's plan for her and her people. She took a deep breath and with her pen she wrote to Mordecai, "I will do it. If I die, I die. But please have our people fast and pray for me because I'm so scared."

Esther prayed for favor in the eyes of the King, and when she had gathered her courage, she cautiously stepped into the King's throne room. She was shaking, knowing that the King could order her to be killed at any moment. She let out a deep sigh of relief when the King held out his golden scepter, giving her permission to approach him. She had found favor in the King's eyes, just as she and her people had prayed for! The King said to her, "What can I give you? I will give you anything you wish – even up to half of my Kingdom!"

As a tear fell down Esther's face, she told him the real reasons she came to see him. She told him about Haman's plan, that she was an Israelite and she begged him not to let Haman destroy her people.

The King fumed with anger toward Haman and ordered that a banquet be thrown in Haman's honor, in order to trap him and arrest him at the party. When Haman walked into the banquet, his head was held high with arrogance and pride. But Haman's mouth dropped open in shock when the King announced to the guests that Esther was an Israelite and that Haman would be arrested for trying to kill the Queen. Haman was afraid and tried to make excuses for what he had done but was quickly marched out of the room to his death.

Esther, Mordecai and all of the Israelites celebrated because their lives had been spared that day. God had indeed brought Esther to Persia to make her Queen so His people could be rescued!

Even today, every year, the Israelites celebrate Esther's bravery and God's love for His people. They feast for two days on delicious food and give each other gifts with hearts of thanksgiving because they were saved from death.

One day, we too will feast, with the King of Kings – Jesus! When we enter the gates of heaven, we will celebrate, with God's SHEroes and all of His people, the victory that Jesus won for us through His death and resurrection!

Devotion:

Do you want to be one of God's SHEroes? If yes, then let's pray...

"God, I believe in you. I believe that you sent your son Jesus to die for me because you love me so much. Thank you that Jesus rose from the dead and that He speaks to me today! Help me to hear you when you talk to me. Help me to be brave when you ask me to do something. Help me to have eyes to see those who need help. Help me to trust you and to know you more every day. Jesus, I want to be your SHEro! Amen."

"And now, O LORD God, I am your servant; do as you have promised..."

2 Samuel 7:25